Timmy ~~teur~~ Polat Lean

Weekly Reader Presents

What Do Doozers Do?

By Michaela Muntean · Pictures by Sue Venning

Muppet Press
Henry Holt and Company
NEW YORK

Copyright © 1984 by Henson Associates, Inc.
Fraggle Rock, Fraggles, Muppets, and character names are trademarks of Henson Associates, Inc.
All rights reserved, including the right to reproduce this
book or portions thereof in any form.
Published by Henry Holt and Company,
521 Fifth Avenue, New York, New York 10175

Library of Congress Cataloging in Publication Data

Muntean, Michaela.
What do Doozers do?
Summary: The Fraggles can't understand why the Doozers love to work and build.
[1. Puppets—Fiction.   2. Stories in rhyme]
I. Venning, Sue, ill.   II. Title.
PZ8.3.M89Wh 1984   [E]   83-22709
ISBN 0-03-071091-X

Printed in the United States of America

What Do Doozers Do?

SOMETIMES, a Fraggle or two may stop to wonder why Doozers do the things they do. But Fraggles could never understand—not in a million, trillion years— that Doozers love to build and work.

Far below the Fraggle caves and halls, Axle Doozer is asnooze in his bed. All Doozers make sure they get plenty of rest, because Doozers need lots of energy.

Forklift Doozer wakes up very early, but he is not the first one out of bed. Other Doozers are already wide awake and busy doing things that Doozers do in the morning.

Molly and Toggle Doozer have breakfast with their three babies, Doodad, Gadget, and Thingamabob. Then off to work they go. One thing Doozers do *not* do is waste time.

A little Doozer needs to learn how to do the things a grown-up Doozer does. That is why all little Doozers go to school. Today, Professor T-Square is teaching them how to build a tower.

Every Doozer also goes to F.A.S. (that's short for
Fraggle Avoidance School). Doozers must know how

to work around noisy Fraggles who always seem
to be having a party or practicing silly tricks.

Throughout all of Fraggle Rock, Doozer building crews are always hard at work. Beneath the Gorgs' garden, Cogwheel and Camshaft Doozer cut radishes and grind them into dust. Treadmill Doozer sends the radish dust down to the factory, where it is molded into Doozer sticks.

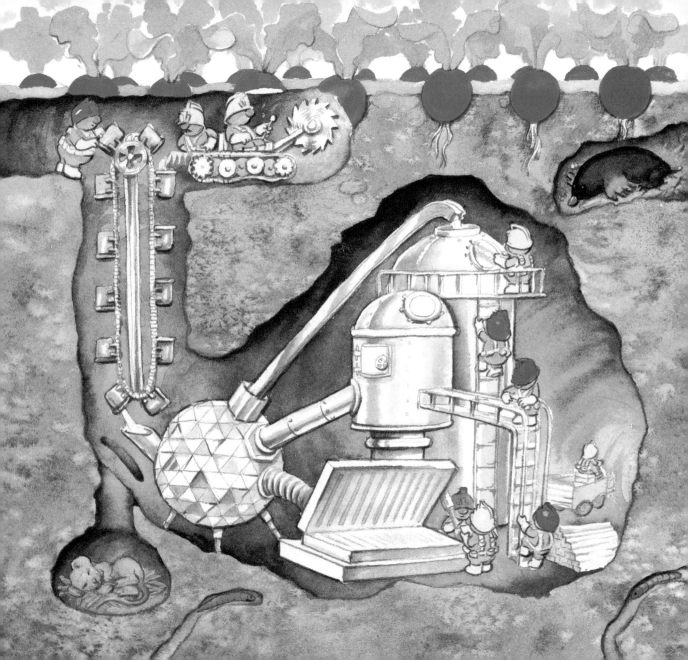

Spike and I-Beam Doozer watch Wembley Fraggle carefully. They are testing a new Doozer stick flavor—rutabaga radish—and want to make sure Wembley likes it. If Fraggles did not eat up Doozer constructions, there would be no more room to build.
What would Doozers do then?

There would be no need to make Doozer sticks,
because there would be no room for new roads or

bridges or towers. There would be no reason for Doozers to get up in the morning at all!

Doozers do not mind if they have to build over, or around, or under something big that happens to be in their way. Doozers will find a way to do it.

A Bull Doozer is leading a construction crew on to build a new bridge, while other Doozers are busy putting the finishing touches on a tower. Sledge Hammer and Pick-Axe Doozer are taking a beezleberry tea break while they discuss plans to build a tunnel under the east wing of Fraggle Rock.